Berto, 3, and Big Red

# Skeleton of a Bridge

by
Robert Mirabal

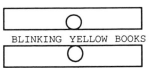

BLINKING YELLOW BOOKS

*Taos, New Mexico*

ISBN 1-883968-02-X

Cover photo by Burt Harwood ca. 1920,
courtesy of The Harwood Foundation Museum,
Taos, New Mexico.

Inside photo (of Robert as a child)
by Geri Mirabal ca. 1969.

Back cover photo by Seth Roffman.

The story beginning, "I was seventeen in the fall of
'61..." was inspired by the cowboy poem,
"The Sierry Petes" by Gail Gardner.

The publishers would like to thank
the Martin Foundation and S.O.M.O.S.
for their support.
And special thanks to Bob McCann.

Blinking Yellow Books is a non-profit publishing house
for the benefit of writers. Contact us at
P.O. Box 3225, Taos, NM 87571

First printing: 1994

## Author's Statement

The stories and characters in this book are in my heart, tapped in by memories of my past.

Somewhere in all of us there is Pumpkin, Browny, Scoop and Gregory playing with the pain, joys and love of our hearts

for the scientists, philosophers, doctors, holy men and women, runners, and comedians of Taos Pueblo

Starchy Montoya was a normal looking kid at seven, but during the school year his Momma starched his Levis, made them sound like a paper bag when he sat down, so all the kids called him Starchy.

School had not started yet, we were on summer vacation, and so Starchy and I tried to extend the last few days of summer into weeks. Even though it had been raining for the last two days, every morning Starchy came over early to my grandparents' summer house; he sat in the kitchen with them. I looked out of my warm blankets and could see Starchy eating oatmeal and tortillas with steam coming out of his well-worn, mildewy clothes. His Momma had already shaved his hair off for school, and he always scratched his bristly neck. I got out of bed, ate oatmeal with them. Grandma was mad at all the rain and the mud because the house and the roof always leaked at the same place every time it rained hard. Starchy said, "Grandma, the rain is good! The Spirits of the Mountain are happy we got Blue Lake back. That's why it's been cloudy and rainy all over: that's what my Dad said." His Daddy was on the Warchief staff, and the staff had killed some buffalo so that they could feed all the people at the celebration for winning back our holy lands. Grandma had helped to cut meat with Starchy's mom.

We got on our bikes and rode into the Pueblo. At the east side wall we stood leaning on our bikes. Starchy had an orange modified Chopper with a silver banana seat. Starchy said he was going to customize mine into a Chopper, too. We just had to get to the dump to look for an old bicycle, "to get the forks off of," he said.

"Hey, look at all the people in line to eat buffalo," said Starch. There were black people in raincoats, white people with brightly colored umbrellas, Indians and Spanish folks holding up cardboard and plastic bags to keep the rain from soaking them, all these people in a line from the race track to the middle bridge, talking, smiling, laughing, having a good time because the people of the small nation they had helped had won over the government. There were white people in line in shiny black shoes and suits, staring at the dark brown wet adobe walls.

The Elders praised a man by the name of Nixon, the President of the United States, who signed the piece of paper that said that the land is Taos Indian land, and it shall always stay wild. For sixty-four years Governors from the Pueblo had fought hard to gain the land back, every year going back and forth to Washington.

Starchy and I knew Blue Lake was holy land. We didn't know who Nixon was; we didn't know all the hard-to-understand situations.

And we sure didn't know who all the people in line were. They walked under an arbor with an American flag that was soaking wet and hung heavily on a white cedar-post flagpole.

"Hey, look at those A.I.M. guys," Starchy said, with a lip-protruding gesture. "Dad said guys from the American Indian Movement were going to be here, so I've got my knife here." He pulled out a thick old antique-looking knife with a screwdriver, spoon, fork and saw on it. I looked at the A.I.M. guys. There were three of them with long hair, bell-bottoms and Levis jackets. Maybe they were A.I.M.. I didn't know what an A.I.M. guy looked like. Some Elders at the Pueblo didn't care too much for them; they thought they were radical Indians from the cities, starting trouble all over. I didn't care. The three guys looked harmless and I didn't think Starchy's thick old knife could have stopped any of them, anyway. They just looked like guys wanting to eat fresh buffalo.

Starchy and I got on our bikes and headed for the dump to look for old bicycle forks.

I thought about the holy land, I thought about the man called Nixon, and about the heavy, wet American flag. I guess America is good, I thought. It gave our land back to us. But I was just seven years old, hardly traditional yet, and maybe I will understand the man Nixon, America, and the holy land when I get older.

What was important now was catching up to smelly Starchy Montoya and riding to the dump to look for old bicycle forks to make me a modified Chopper with a white banana seat.

"Sniff it," Tony said. "No way, I ain't gonna sniff it," said Watermelon. "Let's get Freddy-the-Frog. He'll sniff the hell out of it," said Big Ben. It had been a boring morning, and a lot of us boys had ditched school and planned to go swimming, hang out, and maybe roll a few horseshit cigarettes, and dare each other to inhale the smoke. But things changed. Snuffy, the fat half-breed, had told our plan to his father last night, and now the Principal waited down at Dusty Elk's pond, in a brown Ford pick-up truck. So, our plans changed. We were all in a run-down corral throwing horse dung into a rusty old coffee can, trying to figure out what to do, because Big Ben had just broken the basketball hoop we'd made out of the ol' coffee can. "Slam dunk," he said, with a big horseshit in his hand. He was standing on a Pepsi-cola crate that couldn't hold him, when he jumped toward the wall of that corral and, when he fell, his T-shirt got caught on that

6

rusty can and he ripped it down. He started crying and went on home to his mom, and gave us the blame like he always did. So it was Tony, Freddy-the-Frog, Watermelon and me, bored to the bone in that dusty old corral, sitting on our towels.

We were all having a drawing contest, on the dirt, to see who could draw the best buffalo, deer, and Chevy. It was then, when Tony was clearing himself an area to draw on, that a fat stinkbug came crawling out from one of them piles of horse droppings. We all ran out, leaving Tony on the ground next to that black bug. Tony slowly got up and spat at it, hitting the ground and piss-ing off that big smelly bug, which put its behind in the air, giving off an ol' mildewy smell to that corral. Watermelon, a small, beady-eyed boy said: "Smell it," in a mis-chievous way. Freddy-the-Frog, a skinny boy, who could run like the wind, said: "Shit no, you smell it! You look like one anyway. Relatives, probably!" We all

7

laughed and dared Tony to go in after our towels. Tony wasn't too bright. He was strong though; kicked all four of us around. He was older but hung out with us fourth graders, 'cause he flunked third grade or something. Tony held his breath as he cautiously went in. He grabbed the towels and ran out, tripping on an old rake and flying into the weeds, dirt, and dust. We all ran over to help. When we pulled him out, he had a baby bottle in his hand, full of money. As I grabbed the bottle, Watermelon jumped me and took it away, and Tony tripped him and gave him a quick punch in the arm, making him let go of that pink baby bottle. We all sat down next to each other and counted that money. There was about twenty-five dollars and some change, I think more money than I ever saw at once in my young life.

So the wild bunch planned to walk into town. It was about three o'clock when we neared the plaza, and we were all hungry.

So we went into the Plaza Cafe and had some hamburger baskets and coffee, Watermelon had an Orange Crush soda. We went looking around in the shops and sat in the plaza and stared at the white people and their cars. We all wanted to buy one but we decided on some tennis shoes we saw at Gon-mar's. Black basketball shoes with three white stripes on their sides. We were going to buy socks too but we wanted to go to the movies.

Some Western movie was on, and we all sat in the back row of the Plaza Theater, throwing popcorn at two young couples in the fourth row. When we got out, it was dark already. Watermelon was afraid, almost cried and made us scared too, but we didn't show it. We kept talking about that adventure movie. Slowly, the town's lights disappeared as we walked in the dark back home. We tried to sing cowboy songs, like the ones in the movie. We were the best of friends and, at that moment, time was endless. It was the best day I ever had, and forgetting my Mama's towel in the theater didn't matter. We reached the pueblo and Tony still had some money, that he split with us so that we could give it to our parents just in case they got angry at us. We all agreed that it was the best day we ever had. As I went home I got to worrying about what Mama would say. Then it left me for good when I felt that money and could see them white stripes on my new sneakers glowin' in the dark. I was a man I felt like, a little man with no worries.

Hot July, summer of '73. Nighttime stars twinkle into the velvety dark. Silhouette of the giant Douglas Fir trees shadow the faces of laughing boys. Rattle of pots and pans, the sound of cold, Rocky Mountain rivers. Elroy, Charley and me out camping, on a July weekend. Middle of summer vacation and no worries, mate... Brown-skinned Indian boys, inventing the fart game. Van de Kamps, Van de Kamps, pork and beans. Too many granola bars, fry breads, Gummy Bears, Oreos, ramen noodles, Twinkies, Twix, and too much beef. Late at night in that big canvas tent. Fire barely flickering, suffocating itself, coughing up a flame here and there, then slowly dying into smoke. It was then the fart game was invented.

Charley let one go in his sleeping bag; "snuck up on me," he said, "tried to hold it back until I relaxed..." It was so bad he ran out of his sleeping bag, knocking over fishing poles, dirty pots and empty bean cans, and groceries. Smell seemed to sit heavy in that old canvas tent, on that hot summer night. Elroy and I had covered ourselves under our cheap, synthetic sleeping bags. We couldn't stand it anymore. When Elroy let one go under that sleeping bag, a loud, hard one that woke up the dog sleeping with him in his bag, Dog started whimpering, so Elroy let him out, letting the smell travel out into the air. I couldn't stand it anymore, so I crawled, in my sleeping bag, to the nearest fresh air vent. That old canvas tent had gone through a lot, but not this, I don't think...as I let out a sneak attack fart; not so loud, but deadly. We all ran outside, laughing, and trying to hold our farts in. Elroy started again, then Charley, then I had one of those jalopy sounding ones. Soon the whole camp smelled of cheap junk food, and I didn't feel so good. The only ones near the tent were the dogs. Then they started farting, we could hear them go at it.

We told Charley to get our sleeping bags, since he'd started it.  That old canvas tent was air tight, and he knew it. But he went in, anyway. Soon as he went in, Elroy and I closed the flap door. Charley started screaming in there; started to cry, when we finally let him out. We were laughing so hard that Charley grabbed me and threw me in the tent, and quickly closed the flap door. It was my turn in the smell of horrors house. I could hear the two laughing, in between almost choking and throwing farts. I crawled out of an opening in the flap. I let some go before I got out of that old canvas tent. Charley and I grabbed Elroy and stuffed him through the opening. He was screaming in there, and then his screams diminished to whimpers, and then stopped altogether.  He had fallen asleep with all the dogs snuggled around him.

It's been fifteen years now. Elroy has two kids and is living in the big city. Charley just got married this summer, pretty little

Indian girl, still lives on the reservation, but I hardly ever see him. Strange how you just stop being in contact with smelly friends. And me, I'm still hopping on a horse, going camping whenever I can...Lying here under the stars. River rapids keeping time with a willow branch, caught in the rocks, trying to get free, getting caught by the water, again and again. It's quiet up here, but I can still picture us boys, laughing and running around in our long underwear, that night we invented the fart game.

It had been a regular December morning, meaning waking to the soft chuckle of my grandparents telling each other their dreams in between swallows of tortilla, eggs and spam in the adobe front room of our winter house. It had been in October that we moved back into the Village, inside the walls for the cold months ahead. Everyone knew that their homes would be warm with just a small fire. With all its mud bricks, and with constant plastering, every summer, it was a warm place to live in the winter months. I could smell the piñon wood burning in my Grandma's wood stove, and I could tell it had to be a cold morning, since I could faintly smell kerosene, that my Grandma had started the fire with...usually it was just the smell of burning piñon. I daydreamed and chuckled to myself, imagining how she got the Safeway milk carton she keeps the kerosene in, and with it poured the kerosene on the wood, and then, with no second thought, struck one of those strike-anywhere matches, and with a single hand motion throwing in the match...poof! I chuckled and eventually, slowly got up and put on my favorite Levis and Converse tennis shoes. It's funny; no matter how cold or muddy, we children always seemed to wear our tennis shoes, because without tennis shoes, you couldn't play in the small Day School gym. It looked like a dust storm in the middle of a hot Taos summer in that gym, because all the kids had the same idea: if you had tennis shoes on, it didn't matter if they were full of mud from walking to school or not, as long as you had your tennis shoes on...

Slowly, I stood up and walked across my grandparents' bed, the mattress on the floor, and then into the warm kitchen. I greeted my Grandma, Grandpa. We talked about how we had slept, what we had dreamt of, and of small things that were talked about during the night. I was going outside to do my nature's business. I got my Grandpa's old flannel, red-checkered, button shirt. I went outside thinking of how cold this morning was, compared to the other mornings. I thought that surely, winter has come upon us, to slumber upon our village once more. There was the usual, distant bark of a dog on the south side, and from far on the north side, outside the walls, a power-saw. I thought it was probably Carlos Archuleta cutting at his pig house again for firewood. I came upon the ash pile on the north side, and could see the road leading up to the canyon, and I wondered about the single set of tire tracks going up the road, and about who had gone up to go hunting this morning. I daydreamed, looking at the huge ash pile, covered with snow, and imagined its mound being a mountain top, where all the deer lay quiet on the other side. I slowly climbed up the 'mountain' and saw that it was a stray dog, probably a split between Doberman Pinscher and Poodle, licking an old potted meat can somebody had thrown out. I carefully made a snowball and threw it at the dog, which yelped, even though the snowball had crumbled into a million pieces, not even reaching its destination.

I was coming back and saw old lady Romero baking bread, and saw the heat rising from her oven. I gestured a friendly wave to her, and wondered about Christmas and how good it was going to be this year, because the people had decided to dance the Matachina dance. It had been six years since they had danced it, and everyone was looking forward to seeing it again. I had heard TimoTio Marcus say that, "they found an old man who could play the fiddle just as good as old man Adolfo from Seco, and that his son plays the guitar..." That was one of the reasons they had not danced it in so long--it was because of the death of an old man who was hired to play the fiddle, for a good fiddle player was needed. Every night now on the Indian program, Joseph Romero

would play that old album that Adolfo
recorded of the Matachina dance. And I
could hear my uncle in the next room: "all
right...turn it up..."

The Matachina dance was brought to the
Taos Indians when the Spanish con-
querors came to the new world. It was a
dance of praise for the king of Spain and
his warriors, the Conquistadors. The Taos
Indians adopted this dance to honor Christmas, and the festivities in the Pueblo during those days.

I came near our house and saw that my
Auntie Lou had also built a fire in her oven,
ready to bake her bread. I said: "Good
morning," and then asked her if she was
ready for Christmas. She said she didn't
know but that she was getting ready
whether or not her husband  (my uncle)
was still in jail. I laughed and told her, "I will
see you later." My Grandma and mother
had been waiting for their dough to rise, so

that they could start baking. Funny, I never understood what that meant. I went into the house and could smell the yeast from the dough, and my Grandma already had some pans of dough ready to bake. I went into the back room where I looked at the pretty Christmas tree. It seemed so different, now that it was all decorated. My uncle had gotten the tree for us; a nice gesture, my Mom thought, but I knew that he gave it to us because it was bald on one side so he cut another one for his family and gave this one to us. It didn't matter because it fit perfectly next to the couch. I could smell the tree, and only then did I feel Christmas truly here.

I saw the brightly decorated boxes of presents. I knew that one, the thin, rectangular box, wasn't interesting. I knew it was a box of Brach's chocolate candies that my aunt Daisy always gave us. We all had our presents under the tree, and I imagined them under a blinking Christmas tree like the one Mrs. Green had in her English class at school. Afternoon came, and it was time to go to the corral outside the Village walls, to chop some pitch wood. It was quiet season, and everyone had to do their chopping and cutting outside the Village walls. The pitch wood was for the Spanish bonfires, which symbolized the twelve days of Christmas. Everyone around the Village made their own bonfires. The pitch wood was cut in small, foot-and-a-half long pieces, each placed on top of the other to form a tall square, like a box, or cage. I had cut about two arm loads and had taken it in, next to the house. Steven, my cousin, came out and said: "let's include mine with yours so that we could have a bigger bonfire than Horsehead across." We joked around and we made our bonfire, and sure enough, ours was bigger than Howard Ortiz's. 'Horsehead's'. The bell was ringing and it was time to light them, and as the flames rose, everyone came out. Seems like since I've known Steve, his hair has always been singed in front during Christmas time, because he would jump over the bonfire before his parents could come out and see him.

I saw uncle John. I guess he got out of jail. He'll probably get thrown in tonight again; he doesn't seem to listen. He keeps going down to the Community house where the men are practicing the Matachina, and trying to show them how it's done...

Softly, the reflections on the adobe walls became darker and then all that was left were the red coals, slowly turning into shiny red orange dots that looked like the pictures of cities, and like the town of Taos on a quiet summer night. Uncle John had gone over to Horsehead's brother's, and they had just broken an old screen door, so that they could have more wood to throw onto the fire. I told Steve good night and went inside, hearing Horsehead's brother laugh--he laughed like a donkey, I thought.

I went to bed and slowly fell asleep, wondering at the reflection from the fire on the silver tinsel, which looked like electric Christmas lights, blinking off and on...off and on.

"There's no cranes anymore," said Scoop. "Yeah there is down by the pasture, the place where we caught all those suckers and frogs. They're all over like big flying dinosaurs in the afternoon what are those called, petrroducktails?"

We went down killed a huge Canadian goose right away all the ducks and black birds flew off but the Canadian goose just started running away into the willows. Scoop shot him with his Grandpa's antique 4-10 rifle he snuck out.

Boe-Boe went in after him screaming and screeching his voice was changing and he sounded like a rooster, "You got him, you got him," he squeaked. He ran into the willows started screaming and we ran over to him through the beaver dam...

The goose was chasing him "wah! wah! wah!" the goose screamed...

"Shoot it, Scoop, Shoot it," it was as big as Boe-Boe and it was coming our way...

Boe-Boe jumped into the beaver pond, Scoop shot the goose, killed it, goose white feathery down all over the pond and red willows. A ringing in my ear after the ordeal.

"Get me out of here," said Boe-Boe, the pond was not very deep and it was filled with thick grey black, smelly mud, Boe-Boe crawled out full of big chunks of mud all over his braids and hair. Goose down covered his shining shoulders, we all laughed at him. "Dance," said Scoop, "dance." He went down to the small creek and washed off the mud, his pants stuck to his skin, he peeled them off. Then got into the greasy feeling warm pasture water to wash off.

"Berto, here's the goose," said Scoop, he held it by its web feet...

"Watch I'll imitate Fish Eye doing the eagle dance..." he looked for the wings... "hey where's the wings?" he said, got scared and threw the goose at me..."ahh it's sick his wings are gone..."

We didn't want to touch. Boe-Boe came up the Beaver dam, "what are you screaming about hey where's the dinosaur?"
"It's over there I think it's sick it has no wings."
"No way really let me see," Boe-Boe said, his greasy hair out of his braids made him look like a sun-burnt cave man poking at its prey..."no wonder it couldn't fly."
"No shit Sherlock," said Scoop as he too analyzed it...
"Hey it has a gold bracelet on its foot..."
"Damn, maybe he's a god," said Boe-Boe. "Maybe we killed a god..."
"No way, it's a do-mesticated goose...check it out: says here 100238-F Montana. Hey Scoop, you killed a goose that hitchhiked from Goose, Montana." We all laughed

wondering where it came from, "Maybe
from the slaughter plant," said Scoop, "or
maybe from Jerry Howell's laundry mat..."

"Who cares? let's eat it," said Boe-Boe...
scratching his skinny butt, looking at soggy
matches.
"Damn what if we get caught?" I said.
"For what, killing a goose on Indian land?
Remember we just won back Blue Lake,
beanhead, can hunt anywhere we want,"
said Scoop righteously. "Montana goose
comes hopping along into our land wings
or no wings I'll shoot it..." he went into the
army when he got older, keeps bragging
about Desert Storm at the Sagebrush Inn
when he gets a few beers in him, still can't
take care of his family they all live with her
family...
"OK" I said, "let's cook it, if we take it home
we're going to get caught for sure."
"How come you keep scratching your ass?"
I asked Boe-Boe, "Damn maybe you got a
leech from that horse-shit infested water."

27

"Nah, it's just chapped," he said...
"Still got diaper rash or what?" said Scoop
as he plucked the goose, we always
picked on Boe-Boe because he was so
stupid...skinny accident prone Indian boy
has the best job between both of us now.
"Hey I thought this bird was bigger than
this," said Scoop--after all the feathers and
down were plucked off there lay a pathetic
skinny goose in the coals...

Boe-Boe made us laugh as the wingless
goose cooked...

He put all the feathers in his greasy muddy
hair and held the goose head in his hand...
trying to imitate a story in a movie he saw
at the drive-in, "me Wila-Wakan," trying to
act like a Plains warrior in the movie... "Me
'Man-Called-Horse'" and he acted like he
was doing the Sun-dance...I later in my
years saw the movie on video, gave me a
pretty good laugh thinking about skinny

sunburnt cheeks Boe-Boe trying to tell us
about it that day.

We ate up the goose and Scoop kept the
gold band that was around the goose foot...

Summer Sun was hanging heavy on its
down hill haul, El Salto looked like a
French artist painting beautiful and pictur-
esque, showing off courting with the sun.

Coming back home from crane dinosaur
hunting. Three dark-skinned boys on a
safari, could have been an Anasazi brave,
monkey hunter from South America or a
Masai warrior coming home from a lion
hunt...

"Ahhhh," screamed Boe-Boe, almost
scared the goose out of us.

Scoop lost his balance on the grass
mound he was on, threw his gun into the
tall grass and cattails.

Boe-Boe was crying trying to get his pants off moving his feet like a Flamenco dancer, farting goose farts, "Something biting my ayss, something biting my ayss," he said. Sure enough the leech I pictured, "Turn around," I told him..."I told you it was leech. "

"I thought it was a scab," said Boe-Boe crying trying to look at his behind sounding like a rooster.

Scoop was laughing really hard in the cat-tails looking for his Grandpa's 4-10 rifle.

"Boe-Boe, put your butt in the air and don't fart," I said.

The leech was half way into his skin and part of it was cut from Boe-Boe scratching it..."get me a match," I said to Scoop "and that gold band." I heated up the gold band around a cattail stalk, sun going down, leech knowing somehow that something was up, digging itself into Boe-Boe's butt faster and harder.

Three red-skinned boys in the middle of the west Pueblo high grass pasture one laughing his ass off, one trying to save an ass, one crying, holding his little hairless penis as he screamed out of his rooster voice, a painful yell that made all the horses look up at us and the fifteen crows flying east go the other way...

I branded his butt. The leech squirmed out a bloody zip as it released its blood sucking kiss from Boe-Boe's butt....

He cried until we got to the Pueblo, holding his butt gently walking like he had to drop a load or something ..
"That's what you get for being scared of a wingless goose," I said.
"Yeah," Scoop stoked the flame. "Next time don't imitate a Plains dancer named 'Horse...' " he finally started laughing, then

all of us were laughing by the guide house. People that saw us probably thought we were sniffing gas or something.

Evening came, I left my friends with an appointment for tomorrow, go mountain lion hunting up to Glorietta,
"There's no mountain lion anymore," said Scoop...

We never met the next day or ever again, heart attack killed my Grandpa that night, changed my whole life, changed play time to work, changed my wondering to responsibilities...

I always think about my friends. Scoop, I see him but I don't hang out with him anymore, our roads are gravel going different directions...

Boe-Boe is a lawyer in Albuquerque, a lawyer defending people, with an awesome reputation. I wonder if they'd still choose

him if they knew what was tattooed on his
Indian butt.

Pumpkin had a pellet gun that his Mama got for him at Gambles. Junior had a Daisy BB gun that his Papa got for him at Wacker's. I had a sling-shot that Grandpa helped make, out of an innertube and an old oak prong. My pockets were full of just the right sized stones. Pumpkin had enough pellets. Junior had two boxes of BBs and some in his mouth. We went hunting in the afternoon for anything that moved, birds, horses, cats, silver cans. We were under a big chokecherry tree waiting for the robins to come back and chew some berries when Pumpkin picked up an old bucket to sit on, and a picture of a big, naked lady fell out of it. We just stared at the picture for a spell then grabbed the book. Sat closely around each other and stared, silently as our mouths dried from breathing too hard and deep. We never saw anything like that. Closest was probably when Miss Plum (our intern) went into our Gym class with shorts and a T-shirt, but no bra to show us how to use the trampoline.

The heat of the day subsided and we were still under that chokecherry tree. We laughed embarassed, blushing at all the naked ladies. We turned the pictures into targets and we shot them with Pumpkin's pellet gun, and giggled. We wondered...we wondered...we wondered about women, from then on. We tore the book up but saved some pictures under rocks and old stumps so we could go see the pictures, by ourselves. I saw Junior fold one up and put it in his pocket. We were walking home when Pumpkin made some excuse that he left a pellet box behind and he went back to the chokecherry tree...

We didn't kill no birds or anything that day. We just watched and watched, and wondered and wondered...I would never look at my teachers and classmates the same ever again. My hunting had changed.

Puppy sniffed around the old wooden table where Duke took a piss in the morning. The same old yellow meadowlark yelled out its same old songs on the same old tree. And I pulled up the shade and turned the radio on, put my apron on ready to work on flutes. Same old procedure outside the ancient adobe so-called studio where I create musical instruments.

A dark blue mysterious cloud hovered over the Mountain. Between plum bushes and lilacs a squirrel scurried where there used to be a long pole across the barbed wire fence where its ancestors ran across to get to the pig house, then underneath the decaying vigas by the corral.

I saw April this late morning taking her younger brothers fishing and I guess swimming. I could see them across a field going in and out of my sight, by the old ditch we used to use and the fading chokecherry trees. Her brother carried a fishing pole. The young one carried a stick that he threw at the prairie dogs.

April carried on her back a green backpack maybe change of clothes and a little food for her young brothers. Her floral dress brushing up against weeds in between the trail. Two magpies chased away a bear hawk. To the river. April held her twenty-two rifle loosely. Relaxed. Point drawn to the ground with her right hand.

My worn down hand is greeted by a little black ant looking for food. It climbs my hand up to my fingers gets caught a little bit on my hairs. Analyzes my fresh scars. Falls from my uneven dirty fingernails down to the cedar shavings.

Peering out to the east through the old corn field where there is only stickery rag weed now, the sun brightens a little more on its race.

I hear a gun shot. No echo, a thud that goes into the earth. I see April and her younger brothers running to a prairie dog hole where she has shot at one. The little brother yells out something in Indian, April shoots again, the eight yelping dogs around them barking and digging around at other holes.

Armed woman. Trout woman killed a greasy prairie dog, to maybe cook for hyperactive brothers.

I thought about her today.

Towards the afternoon I saw them running down. Her dark hair that was tied up traditional stuffy flowed with the wind now as she sprinted down farther and farther from her lean brothers. She held her floral dress in her hand not to trip on its hem, and her long black, raw hide soled Indian boots flicked up dust with every step. She looked

like a Pueblo runner training, shaking
bones, stretching sinew.

Sister, Mother forever picking bones to
make elk broth.

Like thunder over the hills, freedom
screamed from her damp hair competing
against the wind. Old woman sewing
maiden boots for your new grand daughter.

She probably thought, I could easily give
anyone a good race. But that thought was
my thought. When it seemed too serious
she stopped and her brothers caught up to
her panting, tired, laughing, brothers and
sisters equal and strong for now.

Afternoon rains were coming, thunder bolts
touched the sagebrush horizon to the west.
I cleaned up my space where Elk flute half
finished lay waiting for me underneath the
green army tarp for the next day.

My last look across the old corn field, where sunflowers grow now, near an old corral, with a wagon with no wheels. April and her brothers reached their mother's house, her thin calloused hands clutching the twenty-two pointing it up to the sky. I wonder if she will take her brothers to hunt again tomorrow.

Dancing outside when no one looks. Practicing to smile the best that you can at a mirror. Clutching today pencils with thin rough hands that tied your brothers' hair. Hunter-Woman, Trout-Woman, Woman-Woman getting on yellow bus to learn how to survive in a Western world.

Rains come, the edge becomes slippery in between the trail where on both sides there are weeds to slip into. Tomorrow we will run again. Tonight I will dream of Elk flute running near Buffalo grass with Brother,

Sister...Where all is equal in the pounding of the earth.

花十 "I remember when I moved back and
tried to look for Gregory. Some music
played softly somewhere on the street
where Gregory lived. An Oak tree lined
road with two small ones at the corner
ends. That's how I remembered it when we
were just kids. Now it had become an over-
ly developed street with too much concrete
and not enough growth. They cut the huge
oak trees that lined the road and planted
some elm trees from China. In one day
they painfully massacred 10,000 years of
the Oak nation on that  street where Gregory lived.

"Gregory was a full blood Taos Pueblo Indian adopted into an Italian middle class
family from Salesbury, Idaho. Immigrants
from the holy Valley of Horses south-due-
west of Rome where ancient ruins look like
Chaco Canyon in the Lazio region. Salva-
toris loved the American Southwest, adopt-

ed a Taos Holy boy. A hyperactive healthy
boy with much liberty. His thick Coke bottle
glasses made him look like a young genius
and chronically nine years old. With no tra-
dition that he could long for except in his
dreams and drawings of beautiful buffalos
and warrior-like braves hunting in snowy
forests and alien looking things he called
kachinas...All of us loved him; besides,
back in the 70s to have an Indian friend
was so cool man.

"When I met him in the summer of 1972 a
cousin of mine wanted to get worms to go
fishing...I remember he said 'Let's go get
worms at Potato Bug Greg's house'--that's
all and I thought this Potato Bug Gregory
guy had a little worm farm. We walked
down the oak tree lined road and other
children were running around towards
Gregory's house. We asked for Gregory at
his house. His Italian momma came out
and told us, he's in the old Tyler barn.

"In the old barn was a bunch of kids in the early morning talking, laughing. Some fat kids, some short kids, some curious skinny-legged kids with fishing poles in their hands. And everyone became silenced when a young dark-skinned boy started talking. His voice echoed in the old barn and all of us became silent and circled the boy like some church ceremony. With long dust-speckled sunbeams breaking and squeezing through the old roof. 'OK my little brothers, come on out potato bugs. OK my little brothers, come on out earth worms. OK my little brothers, come on out of the ground potato bugs.' And to my amazement and all the young kids', coming out in a row, potato bugs shiny brown little bugs, fifteen or so, then about twenty were all around this little arena circled by white boys and magical cere-mony orchestrated by a red-skinned boy. Mildewy smell came out from the earth and the worms came out and crawled around Gregory's long fingers. And my fat cousin

Farley started picking them up and putting
them in his little can for the fishing trip. He
gave Gregory a quarter for the worms, Farley all jolly and still in the light watching the
worms. Smelling like bacon.

"Gregory and I became friends from then
on. He had a gift that not even his adopted
parents understood. After all, all they knew
were Italian Catholic upbringings, lonely
aging Italian immigrant couple with no children adopted a holy baby from the Southwest with a gift from his ancient ways that
he breathed, and cherished somewhere in
between Jesus and boisterous Italian
living.

"That summer was the only time I ever
spent time with Gregory. One day on a
rainy afternoon, lightning touching the horizon, tornado clouds forming overhead, we
sat underneath a bridge with small white
butterflies that took shelter on our hands.
He got up and started chanting and danc-

ing and he looked like an angel pounding the sand and butterflies sang the songs in the wind and the rain kept time on the River drum...

" 'Everyone has a gift from the earth, you have to find it and one day that's what I'm going to do,' he said. I think he already had the gift and he gifted us all in Salesbury, the gift to cherish all creation...

"He wrote to me a few times after I moved away. Mostly on the times when he was disgusted with people treating the earth like a war that someone was to win...and Nobody wins and the earth loses every time. In a sad letter he wrote, 'the potato bugs all died in Salesbury,' he said, 'after the Molybdenum mining spill in '74. And all the worms in Tyler's barn stopped coming out after he sold it. They tore it down and made a shopping mall on top of the Sacred Arena, the Butterfly Cathedral of boys' ceremony and  Gregory led the ceremony on the rainy days of July when the heatwaves stopped, 'because the Ancients told me to do it,' he said. 'When it rains the earth smiles, when it pours creations sing.' What was he? Was I so caught up in my own little world that I could not fully understand? How this boy was so philosophical and alive.

"Then the letters stopped, just stopped forever. I never knew what happened to my friend. Maybe, maybe he found his gift in New Mexico, back in Taos. I heard his Italian parents blew themselves up in a freak propane accident.

"Maybe now he calls out little potato bugs for young red-skinned boys that giggle when they whisper secrets to Gregory that white skin boys never heard. Or did our technology destroy you, Gregory? I don't know...but I wonder where you could be Potato Bug Gregory today when the heat waves are overwhelming. We need the

47

ceremony, we need the dance, because we all forgot, Gregory my Red Skin friend, we forgot the ceremony, and the earth and creations need the life force. Where could you be potato bug. We forgot the ceremony. I forgot the ceremony."

Momma told me a story about my cousin Gregory, someone I barely remember. Momma said, when she worked for Mr. Sausage at the co-op, "a rich couple that he knew from Italy would come and visit him in the summer." My Grandpa and Grandma became pretty good friends with the Italian couple, Grandpa would smoke imported smelly cigars and Grandma would pass out the presents the round jolly lady brought for us. Jackets, berets, macaroni, and Italian spices. The couple did not have any children of their own. Always they did things for us kids. Take us fishing, and pick blueberries, their favorite was Gregory.

From what I can remember Grandma telling me, the Italians asked her if they could adopt Gregory or take him for his 6th grade year to Idaho...

Grandma didn't want to give him up for adoption, Gregory was nine years old and he wanted to go with the Italians they always bought him toys and stuff at Wacker's.

"Know what, Browny?" said Gregory, he always called me Browny, "They're goin' to baptise me in Ayy-duh-ho, the Italians; know what, Browny? They eat tasty snake-looking things in chile soup called spas-ghetti." Seems like a bribe when I think about it now...but we were dirt poor, not enough to eat, always eating Saltine crackers and vienna sausages, colon problem from government-issued pro-cessed food and white flour tortillas.

There were eleven of us in the small sum-mer house. Sunburnt brown-skinned kids helping Grandma and Grandpa weed the corn fields on hot, dusty, Sangre-de Cristo afternoons.

Coming back home from the bean fields to the north. Wind was picking up. Grandpa sweaty and dusty steered the wagon in, being pulled by two old horses, Big Red and Vanilla. Simultaneously breathing hard, swatting late summer horseflies with their long tails. Cousin Gregory was leaving today. The Italians finally bent Grandma's back to let him go for his 6th grade year.

Everyone was crying. Hugging him like he was going to leave us forever, that radical can't-catch-your-breath crying was what big Aunt Lou was getting into, but everything made her cry.

The ponies hung their heads low. Brown puppies stuck their soft warm bodies out of their little cardboard box to see...

The car began to drive off. Gregory waved goodbye, still holding his Indian suitcase: a brown paper bag full of T-shirts, mismatched socks and new underwear. Can't go anywhere with dirty underwear so Grandma got some for him at Gon-mar.

"Big dipper held heavy water," said Grandpa. "It will rain soon." The big glowing sun slowly moved northward to Coyote's ear. Every boy was practicing and training for the races, September 30th, except Gregory, but I am sure he's running wherever he is...the Southside runners will miss their sleek runner...

Gregory never came back after his 6th grade year. Grandma kept asking Mr. Sausage about the Italians and Gregory...They never returned, the letters stopped, the co-op burned down in the winter. Mr. Sausage went to Mexico for the winter; he also never returned, freak accident killed him, I heard a donkey fell on him on some hike...I don't know, but everything after they took Gregory got weird for him. I guess because he lied to Grandma that they were only going

to take him for a while...I later found out it's
called karma.

The swallows called Gregory where he
taught me how to hand-fish by the huge
cottonwood trees. Where the marshland
turned into waterbed-like earth, shaking
and jiggling like Jello, we would run
around everywhere. He had a gift, he could
talk to animals and insects, he tried to
teach me but I forgot the ceremony.

My body became hard and small whiskers
developed under my chin, my voice changed, the Moon had a funny relationship with
Morningstar, and it flirted with Venus year
after year.

In my dreams, screaming aunts, uncles,
and elders slowly walked away from their
holy child, he was gone forever. And we all
bowed to his memory when he was younger just losing his baby fat and his polyester

striped shirt finally fitting over his Indian
belly button. Gregory was gone forever.

*We came from Florida to see the
Southwest art and culture. We saw
something we never want to see again.*

*We saw a young Indian man chase down a
rabbit and beat it while it screamed and
crawled with a broken hip to safety.*

*The young Indian man with his face
painted red looked at us with a stern look.
Picked up the rabbit and with one bloody
stroke to the rabbit's neck killed it, then
went off with his so-called prize. My five
year old saw this, also my seven year old
son. We came from the city where con-
tinuously we try to keep our children away
from the violence, but in this small place
we have seen cruelty beyond belief. Bye
Taos. Bye Savage.*

*signed, Never to Come Again*

First summer rain fell softly last night.
Crickets have gone. I missed their

mysterious songs that they sing late into the night, sometime in the middle of the night I woke up with an anxiety attack where I am out of breath and I feel trapped. Nothing new, it goes away quickly when I get fresh air. The rain had stopped. Dark greyish clouds in spots were crossing and covering a deep blue starry sky.

I opened my window. A cool breeze pushed the smell of rain and coldness into the room and my sheets. Feeling better I snuggled back into my bed rubbing my feet, trying to recover the warmth. Slowly getting warmer, smelling the sweet wet earth. Falling asleep thinking of the rabbit hunt tomorrow.

At daylight I could hear the Warchief's men yelling, telling the initiated men to get ready for the hunt. I made my lunch for the day, got my rabbit clubs ready. I asked Grandpa if it was going to rain. "I don't know," said Grandpa, "Something ain't

right." He had a difficult time with his new
dentures and not having his last lower right
jaw molar didn't help him any. The morning
was getting hot and humid but Grandpa
couldn't tell if it was going to rain probably
would.

My uncle Virgil wasn't going on the hunt.
He was listening to some old Rock and Roll
albums in the back room, his half-breed
wife left him so as usual he moved in with
Grandma. I don't like him, he gave up. He
came staggering one afternoon down the
road drunk to the quick. Chickens and
roosters running all over the place. "God
damn chickens." he said and kicked Grandma's favorite hen--bright squawk, white
feathery chicken football went flying into
the barbed wire fence--killed Grandma's
best egg layer. Kicking that hen caused
him to lose his balance and stagger into
the run-down pig pen. Bunch of boards
with big, rusty, antique nails sticking out of
them. Sank his foot into one of them deep

and good. Lay screaming, nobody was home, nobody heard him. Virgil passed out almost died of blood poisoning. If it wasn't for Blood Deer having the runs and going to the out-house he would probably be dead now.

The guy complains, hates white people, loves their clothes, money and booze. Never had made the proper connection to self. Hates people who don't participate in the kiva. I don't know why, he never goes down, but becomes a holy man in the plaza and Ogelvie's in the eyes of pretty foreign girls.

Anyway he griped to me about being late to the hunt. No comment from my side. I knew he was full of shit (rust).

Many men gathered at the hunt, ceremonial circles that honor the earth and its creations, an ancient way on foot, horses, clubs. The way fathers hunted and honored their existence, their muscle, bones, breath. The animal that gives life from the beginning, Deer, Elk, Buffalo, Bear, Trout, Eagle, Rabbit. And we were there where our heart and soul belong. We made our hunt circles on the Indian land. Took a few life forces. Everyone anticipated the better hunt across the road near the hotels and museums. I remember when there was nothing but a few houses--now cars, buildings, people--built on holy hunting grounds. The anticipation left all by the end of the day, sweaty horses, sunburnt run-ners. Circle after circle, no game, no new life force, the rain clouds never came, the rabbits never came, what prophecy was fulfilled? Why did they pour poison pellets near the big hotels and houses, because they wanted no blood thirsty Savages around when tourists are in abundance, or because they want to control everything? I don't know.

We came home early that day we didn't even sing the happy hunting songs. I didn't want to see my wasted uncle so I went to my Grandpa's traditional house stood on the roof watched the sunset develop.

I thought hard about life, there is a limit beyond which man cannot reorganize the earth and sky, to accommodate to his needs.

A true hawk swooped fast and low to the ground, a fat groundhog tried hard to scamper into its hole home. A dust cloud arose, wings flapped vigorously, then stopped. True hawk lifted itself up into the sky. Hanging from its talons was the fat ground hog. It flew over me sang its happy hunting song. A rain of small droplets of blood sprinkled the dirt roof, blood soaked up the dirt around it and a tiny ant got nutrients from the fresh blood offering and sang, I am sure, its happy hunting song.

Tomorrow will be corn dancing I think I will dance, rain will come again I want it to soothe my sunburnt skin touch my hair to heal, touch my uncle to heal, touch my people to heal, touch the foreigners to heal, touch the earth to heal, touch the animals to heal, tomorrow will be corn dancing I will dance for healing.

It was a sunny Sunday morning in the desolate plains, in 1866. Mickey was a little Irish boy going west with his Grandad, Grandma, and little sister Rosie. Going across the new state of Kansas to Colorado, where his mother and father had a ranch.  On the outskirts of a poisoned waterhole and stretch of thick green buffalo grass, Mickey's Grandma was shot with a Comanche arrow while getting into the old covered-wagon; shot through the neck. She fell on top of Grandad; before Grandad could pick her up, he was stabbed from behind by a young warrior with an elk-bone knife. The Indians left Mickey because they were afraid of albinos, and his little sister Rosie went running down to the poisoned water hole, screaming, shouting, pulling her hair...Little sister Rosie went crazy, and the Comanches left her alone. (It was a sunny Sunday morning in the desolate plains, in 1866.)

Eight hundred acres of cedar post fence
line, fifty miles from Maybell, in north-
western Colorado. Dry, dusty, piñon and
sagebrush covered hills. Philbert and
Sagey. Philbert was a full Irish cowboy.
Sagey was part Whiteriver Apache, and
another form of God's dusty medicine bow
winds. Both were friends to the end.  At
sixteen, they knew they were men--they
had settled well in the saddle and had
ducked many a punch. It was Philbert's
birthday. He got twelve bits from bossman
Menford. They bought a good lunch and a
bottle of hot spirits, and started the trails off
to the vermillion bluffs to catch the Rough
River wild horses.

They came upon them in a washed out
gully; they went on the chase out of the
canyon, into the horizon of sagebrush and
piñon. Philbert had a young Dun take him
back into the wash and Sagey was after a
Roan, heading the herd into the bluffs, fast

63

as that Indian's arrow, and never to be caught.

The Indian was put on the Reservation, his horses left to roam the badlands. The Indian put his soul into the horses: that's why freedom's so important to them horses... They don't want the same fate as their black-haired spirit brothers. Philbert understood this as his yells and whistles stopped...He had ridden in and out, chasing that Dun.

In the east he could faintly see Rabbit Ears Pass, and Mount Ethel. He came to a slow stop and saw that Dun catch up to the others at the bottom of the hill. He couldn't see Sagey anywhere. He went looking for him. It was way past sunset, when Philbert found Sagey's buckskinned Indian pony, lying in the sagebrush dead. It had slipped on a drying water hole that was filled with mud. Sagey had chased wild horses since the pair were eight years old, and they knew all the stories of these wilds...Spirit horses never touching the earth, souls of lost, restless Indian ghosts. They loved hearing them, that's where they were free, free from regrets. Dinosaurs are dead, buffalos and Indians have the same fate... Sagey always said, "When I die, bury me under a cedar, to make shade for a wild horse and to help a fellow cowboy with another fence post, to guard his bounty." In the dirt and rocks is where Philbert found young Sagey, wlth his hemp line lariat in his hand, dead sure as hell, with a broken neck. It was Philbert's seventeenth birthday and he cried, as he buried his half-breed friend in the moonlight.

*dedicated to my cowboy poet friend, Waddie Mitchell.*

"Ain't no more fish in that pool," said
Poof, "New Clorox company killed all
of them, they had a spill the other night.
Pinky found this out when he saw ol' White
Tooth floating around in the debris, dead
as the trees he chewed down. I guess
Pinky started picking up them fish and him
and his family had a fish fry. Now they're all
in the hospital..."

"Is Pinky all right?" asked Joey.
"Sick as hell...But you know something?
Lawyer said they're getting a lot of money."

"Ain't no more fish in that pool," said Poof,
"but a lot of big fish where Pinky fishes...I
think I'll go see him and find out what
Clorox tastes like..."

Freddie said he was leaving home. Papa slapped Mama down the stairs. Freddie said he wants to go to Grandpa Sloan, down the dusty road, across the Interstate not to fish, not to see the old mare at Brown's and not to play with the turtles at Turtlemill. Alcohol and unemployment put Papa in a cage. Dirty dishes and an empty, second-hand refrigerator set Mama to open that well-locked cage. Freddie said he's coming home with Grandpa Sloan to shoot Papa and take Mama away.

We saw the headlights of Grandpa Sloan's old Jeep two nights later. After a spell, the Jeep was gone. No fighting, no shouting, just the purple lightning flashing through the trees lighting up that Cimarron sky. And I never saw Freddie again. Just his Papa, drinking himself to death.

It was the last day of school. Summer vacation. No more teachers, no more homework and no more classes. Me and Missy, Missy and me, we were both half-breeds, mixed up in both worlds. She was my best friend. She protected me, and I would do anything for her. The only space between us came because she was smart, and I could barely figure out the system. We'd sit in the woods at night, talking about life. She asked me once: "What do you want to be when you grow up?" I said to her, "I don't...Maybe more mixed up; a mixed up fireman on the Reservation. No kid really cares these days what they're going to be in thirty years, twenty years-- the world is going to be blown-up any-way..." After a pause, she spoke, "What if it isn't?" she asked.

One night we walked to the movies. Saw an old Elvis film. They never had good movies in town. That night, Missy and I

68

went down to the apple orchards and got
two bushels of apples and hid behind the
big, grey ashpile on the southside. Started
throwing them at cars. You could hear the
hard ones hit the sides of the cars and
echo around the Pueblo. We sat there
laughing until we saw spotlights, flashing
up against the big ashpile. Walking home,
we could hear two little boys laughing in
the night, having a pissing contest over the
dark, adobe wall. We scared them and
chased them into their house.

I didn't find Missy in the following days; I
guess she had gone with her parents
somewhere. I knew I was in love with
Missy. I was too close to being a kid still
secretly playing with G.I. Joes to know what
to do, and she was too much of a friend for
me to even hold her hand. She was pretty,
I knew that much: long hair and a beautiful,
naughty smile; I thought of her lips often,
and of how it would feel to kiss them.

Then Missy came to my house one night, in her Papa's truck. I tried to ask her where she had been and why she had left so suddenly, but she didn't say much. She held my hand in the night. I asked if she wanted to go for a walk; "It's raining," she said, but she got out of the truck and walked with me to the river. The rain stopped and we could hear the raging river and the stones being washed loose. Missy told me that night that she was moving away with her Mama, tomorrow. "Papa drinks too much, and Mama is confused here in this place. She won't let me stay, and you know Papa's reputation. I've thought about it and I have to choose to go with Mama..." The walk back to the truck was long. The moon clawed its way out of the clouds for a last peek at Missy. We sat in the truck, crying and holding on to each other tightly, trying as hard as we could to remember one another. I told Missy I would miss her; she held on to my jacket tightly, and kissed me. That was my first and my last kiss from

Missy. She left me that night; I could still smell her perfume, as I fell asleep crying for my Missy...

She moved to L.A., to the big city. I got a letter from her today; she says she misses the places where we had spent time together. I walked around those places, missing her naughty laughter. Sometimes I could still recapture the feel of her lips touching mine, but that was all.

Summer vacation was almost over. I spent most of it alone. I went fishing; did things a sixteen year old would, and I had to deal with my first broken heart. She left me for good. Writing a letter to her tonight, I looked out the kitchen window to see the headlights of an unknown car, driving around late at night. I sat hoping it would turn this way...Hoping it would be Missy-- once more to make me laugh on this lonely summer night.

I was seventeen in the fall of '61 and I was going to school in Kansas, learning about refrigeration and accounting. Don't know how I got started; no one had electricity back home to own a refrigerator, and my accounting wasn't going to help anyone either. Taos was almost poverty stricken, third world country in America.

I was in Nevada Hall, ready to bunk down, when Willy Moon came crashing into the dormitory. He was a skinny Cherokee boy. Long, greasy hair, big ears. Bizarre boy, with a windy knack for finding bones and long-gone things of the past; he would be playing baseball, slide into third, and come up with a shaved knee, while on the ground, all covered in dirt and blood would be a flintstone arrowhead. He even brought into Biology class, for extra credit, a real skull that he found in Buddy Dreadful-water's driveway, near Coonsville Auto-VU drive-in. He thought it was a container of some kind. He kicked it out of the earth, almost broke his skinny big toe.

So then, Willy dragged me outside to tell me that he and Billy Joe Candy, a big, husky hard-living half-breed, had been under Boomer's Bridge drinking cheap wine, when they heard a car drive across the bridge, and then stop in the middle. Now both of them were pretty drunk, and crawling out from under that bridge wasn't easy. This man on top kept on teasing them, telling them to "....dig a deep hole to hide in, and just stay down there, and sit and drink beside the river like stupid dumb Indians do best!" I admit, Billy Joe Candy wasn't too bright, but you dare not tell him that. And he could be a down-right sleuth when the time called on him to be. He was really mad, Willy said his nose was turning pale with every step. When they got out from under the bridge, there stood a man in a long, dark coat. Billy Joe and Willy walked up to this mystery man who had made fun of them. Something was strange about this man, for when he dropped his coat and turned around to tell them, you should've stayed under the bridge, "...this wasn't a man," said Willy, "He had furry legs and feet like a goat, big pointy ears, a long willowy tail, and horns." It was the Devil himself that these two Indian boys met on Boomer's Bridge. He pranced around the bridge and his tail whipped up dust, shouting: "I come from Hell's dry, twisting canyons, and I'm in need of some fresh, blanket-assed souls..."

Willy said he ran down the bridge, thinking Billy Joe would do the same, but Billy Joe was mad at that old Devil for calling him a stupid Indian. When Willy turned around at the end of the bridge, all he saw was Billy Joe deck that son of a bitch onto the ground of that bridge. Billy Joe Candy K.O.d the Devil with one punch, and the Devil was still out cold when Willy and I rode over to Boomer's Bridge. We all

stared at that calloused looking thing. We
tied him up, shaved his hair, clipped his
smelly goat hooves and painted them pink;
even painted his horns pink, too. Then,
tattooed him with a hot hanger on his back,
with: "Dumb Indians did this!" We cut his
thick tail off, it looked like a mean old pit
bull's tail all stubby, then we threw him into
the river. Willy's dog got the tail before we
ever sent it away to the Mormons, like we
had planned. That was back in 1961 when
I was seventeen.

But if you're ever near Boomer's Bridge
and you hear a scary mournful cry, it's that
old Devil in a fit of weeping for his lost tail.
And you know who tattooed him.

It was a hot, humid Tahlequah afternoon as usual. Stubbs and I had been
to the Strawberry Festival Parade earlier
that morning in Stillwell. Stubbs picked up
Lucy, a Choctah girl. We piled in the Buick
and went to my house for a cold brew, to
conquer the dust in the throat.

Stubbs knew he loved Lucy, but sometimes he didn't know what to do, since he
was seventy-five pounds way overweight. I
don't think he cared and neither did Lucy, I
figured. But who gave somewhat of a
damn, were her parents in Okmulgee: a
respectable family that worked with the
government.

We were drunk from ear to ear by that
afternoon, from cheap green bottled wine,
and we turned into three, greasy-faced
gargoyles, sitting on cheap Walmart lawn
chairs, with mosquitos all around us.

Now Stubbs loved Lucy, and I figured Lucy
did too...He adjusted his sights on me and
said: "let me tell you, Berto, I've been reading this here Indian book and it says that a
long time ago a young buck like me got
himself a good woman by going out on
horse raids, capturing horses, and giving
them to the father...buffalo skins, hides, and
such things too. What do you think, Berto:
me and Lucy here?" Lucy smiled at me. I
didn't think much about them. I thought
more about the big new silver capped tooth
that Lucy got at the Indian Hospital. "Go for
it!" I said. I knew that Stubbs loved Lucy
since he was in grade school, and had that
worm farm by her Papa's cornfield. I asked:
"What are you going to trade for her...
worms?" "No, no!" Stubbs said, "You see,
Berto, I got me a whole house full of government issued food. I got commodities to
trade for a good woman; I got commodity
beans, commodity beef stew, commodity
shortening, good for crispy fry-bread,
commodity all-purpose flour, and, not to

mention commodity cheese--probably fifty pounds of that stuff. They issue it to me at Sequoia Indian School every Tuesday. I told them I have ten kids and live way up in Keetoowah Country...Fooled the Government, eh Berto? Trade like the old way, eh Berto?" I didn't know what to say--just took another swallow of that cheap wine. I knew one thing: they both were in love...

The night slowly came, the stars spread across the sky; some shot from one end to the other, and I could hear Stubbs and Lucy make wishes. I passed out sometime in the night. I felt Lucy put a quilt over me. I glanced down the road, the blue moonlight shone through the end of a heart-shaped cave of oak trees. In the middle of the cave were Stubbs and Lucy, holding hands in the summer moonlight...Now Stubbs loved Lucy, and I figured plainly that Lucy did too...

It snowed last night in the full clear moonlight, quiet, glowing snowflakes that fell in slow motion. Sometimes that happens in Taos: snows on a perfectly clear day or clear night. One of those magical nights when sagebrush tops look like thick fluffy cotton balls with shiny crystals that reflect the huge moon. Airplanes left smoky long snake-like trails across the sky.

Over by the river where the gigantic cottonwood trees are, I could hear the soft river muffled underneath the thick ice...where you and I played ice hockey in the middle of the night sneaking out of the house meeting my Pueblo puppy love, Iris...

"What do you want for Christmas?" I asked you, such an ancient question I always ask you every Christmas, every year and always the bleak stare comes across you because maybe this guy can't afford a trip to some island far away where the deep blue sea welcomes you warmly. "Maybe a trip to some island where there's orchards of beautiful wild red, blue, yellow flowers, where hummingbirds and butterflies chase each other. That's what I want for Christmas," you said jokingly. "Some island where I can play on the warm sand where my pueblo body can touch the ocean waves and where I can hold my head up, my hair be caressed by the palm tree winds. Somewhere just once, one time I would like to go when Taos Pueblo and the haunting Taos Mountain is covered with thick cold shivery snows. I could be drinking pineapple juice from a coconut like Ginger on <u>Gilligan's Island</u>, underneath the blazing glorious island sun..."

I saw your face, so clear, so light, like a child in your expressions talking about some fantasy island Christmas wish. But I knew you too well, Iris, I knew simple pleasures of life, honesty and happiness with yourself and others were more important. Ever since you were a little girl I could remember you taking care of your alcoholic father making him Indian tea and white bread toast, looking into the light of candles washing dishes spacing out with dreary eyes you thought of a fantasy on an island where you one day would see and feel.

Years passed and we separated in the spring. I wonder where you went, if I knew, maybe I would send you flowers that bloom in the winter...because they bloom red and you liked red flowers and it don't matter, maybe it does now, everyone loves roses you like simplicity...Poinsettias that bloomed in your pueblo kitchen, when thick snow fell in the sunshine of a Christmas Eve morning. Seeing you upstairs opening the skylight of your pueblo home, dirt roof turning into mud, icy grasslands to the west looked like a piece of glass.

Let me see your long silky black hair get tangled, mixed up with the flowery innocent snowflakes. Let me see you run in happiness chasing devilish runaway flakes that swiftly get twisted in the wind, that catch your eye and melt on your lovely warm Indian face, sneaking out making snow angels at the Day School playground... grabbing icy swings freezing on your fingers...

I thought of you last night, as I came out of the sagebrush trail close to my adobe home. Cold toes, frozen boot soles, heavy breath like a smoke signal slowly left my mouth collapsing breath pushed down, earth bound by the cold.

West by the dry gulch I could hear coyotes crying, the crispy air made the sound travel far. Looking up into the Taos Mountain, I saw a falling star shoot in two directions, the kind that leaves a glow in the sky after it stops. You could see pieces of it falling off,

maybe it was one coming through the iono-
sphere, breaking off in two when it hit the
atmosphere. I thought maybe it's easier to
fall in love with what doesn't last forever.
Maybe it's weird but I fell in love with
shooting star.

My small adobe house, a little reminder of
paradise that we tried to create, some de-
cision made by us. Just too young, that's a
good excuse for lost children trying to find
and be each other's better parents. I lit a
yellow candle, small friendly light filled the
bed area, I stoked the piñon logs that seemed to lie warm and comfortable in the antique stove...

Lying down to sleep, smelling the piñon
wood smoke that crept out every once in a
while from a hole in a stove pipe. I thought
about Iris--she has two twin girls in third
grade, calls them Twinkies. Abusive un-
decided Pueblo husband. Beat up brown
Hudson. Greasy hair. Beer drinking gut.

Thinking about a Christmas gift you told me
about a long time ago, flickering yellow
candle and the island you spoke of came
alive in you like you had been there, some
fantasy island Christmas wish that you
never saw and that I never gave you, some
fantasy island Christmas wish that came to
life in both of us when we were young.
Now every time during Christmas when
candlelight teases the dark and comforts
me on icy cold nights, a Northerner wind
blows crystal snowflakes on adobe homes,
constantly gives me memories. Sagebrush,
valleys to the east and I, you both fall
asleep with deep dreams of some fantasy
island that we both know, but never saw...

Great Grandpa told him that he was going to marry a white lady. He had blue eyes, and light complected skin, that got sunburned in the summer. He was a full blood Indian, and all the girls were after him. Grandpa was right. He married some lady, with blonde hair and green eyes. He had two children: Scotty and baby Jess. He started drinking and beating his wife--a shadow of what his papa did to his mama. He was a hell raising, peyote chewing, blue-eyed Indian. Hung out with some Hell's Angel bikers from northern New Mexico. "Mountain Rats #1," he spray-painted on his mama's adobe wall. She cussed and carried on. Finally got the Bureau of Indian Affairs after him. They caught him stoned, and drunk, passed out under the shade of huge cottonwood trees that were full of pigeons. They took him to a detox center to get help for his drinking. He learned to paint, and to make silkscreened

T-shirts. He made them all for his biker
buddies.

Years went by with him terrorizing his family; his wife left him and went East, to get
educated. He came over to the house often. He listened to Van Halen with us and
told us prison stories. How he killed Ponca-
Sioux in Breckenridge, whose friends were
still after him. He never was in prison and
has never been to Breckenridge--he just
liked the name, and 'Ponca-Sioux' were
just random names of tribes he talked
about. It could've been Cherokee-Pima,
Blackfoot-Crow; today it was Ponca-Sioux.
Then he would talk to Grandpa. They'd
both go into the old, run-down shack, and
he'd cry all over Grandpa's shoulder about
how bad he was, how hard it was for him
and that he would try to get better and
when he was, he said, he would come to
Grandpa and help us with the fields and
dig the old well out for us, so we could
have running water nearby. He never did.

I wasn't at his second marriage, he got married at the Courthouse. Indian boy married a Swedish girl, blue eyes like his. Not as fat as him, but a tall lady who liked his walk, and could tolerate his mess. I saw him one night at a party, with his wife. I could see his fat cheeks sunburned, I saw his blue eyes shed a cold tear down his cheek, into his mouth. He cried on my shoulder now, about Grandpa's death. I knew he missed him and so did I. He told me he would come help me out with the family, and maybe together we could dig out the old well, so we could have running water nearby. I knew he wouldn't, but I hugged him close to me anyway, 'cause I missed Grandpa, and the old times.

It was a pretty summer night. Franky came home from Chicago. Eight years. Hard to believe we were both just kids when he left. Well, I guess kids, somewhat. He was in love with home, and back home was not south Chicago. South Chicago wanted him home; south Chicago had Franky by the hair, and was jealous of home. Gold Glessner Warrior from south Chicago, Lieutenant #T. 5-53. He hated Chicago. He was tired of the Chicago skyline and of the sick smell of Lake Michigan. He couldn't pull out and I knew it. He was in the army--the army that this city of big shoulders breeds in its children. Just another gang in a home of a hundred streets and walls.

"...We own people, streets, cars, buildings, women, families, you name it...If you thought about all the shit you saw around these places, you would go crazy some-

times...ain't worth thinking about... Yes, I
sell rock, Mr. Brownstone, you've heard it
all...Drugs, women, and money..." He
stopped talking. Took a long drag of his
cigarette. Continued: "...but I'm on R and
R...Rest and relaxation for one week, and
nobody's taking that away..." But he knew
south Chicago was jealous, and for one
week he loved home every morning, every
night, every day. The last night with home it
rained a little. The dirt roads glistened, and
the puddles down Grandma's road reflected the moon and stars.

Franky took the train early the next day,
back to Chicago. He told me he would be
back for the Christmas holidays. I didn't
know if he would or not; he lived a day at a
time. He loved home and home loved him;
he knew south Chicago was jealous. And
he knew the whore, south Chicago, had
Gold Glessner Warrior #T.5-53, by the hair.

Tony washed the blood from his hands in an aluminum bucket and Alison just looked on crouched next to the bucket and a Chevy truck, her hair was dusty and the stifling wind blew it into her face, shapely Indian girl with brown hair and a front tooth she lost from a fight with her small Mexican husband a long time ago... reminds her of wasted fruitless years when she was in high school.

And Tony was a Navajo bull rider full of shit and bull, bull shit that never ends, his burly body naive face didn't match his girlish voice...now a man lay dead next to a dead pig, coagulated blood and splattered brains stained the Navajoland corral on the northern territory closer to the Hopi Reservation.

Tony threw the bloody water on the dead man and the water soaked up in his old Levis and thin T-shirt and some dripped

90

slow motion next to his head from the top of his black greasy hair down a bloody strand. On top of his ear it collected there and drip, drip, drip...Alison looked at this, between blinks of her eye she played with the bloody drips, blink drip blink drip blink.

"Let's get out of here," shouted Tony, his girlish voice no one took serious neither did Alison. She slowly stood up reached over to the dead man and stole from the earth the last watered down bloody drip... She turned slowly and her skinny neck muscles flexed when she opened her mouth and tasted a drop of greasy blood. "Let's go," she said as if she were the one waiting, she sat in the truck and remembered where they met...Somewhere in Albuquerque and that's all she remembers and that's all she cares to remember...from one crime job to the next robbery mostly just to get gas and maybe some junk food, pork rinds that they loved...Alison was caught in an undertow now torn and

91

twisted not knowing where the land was,
she was caught her weak vulnerable faith
was caught by Tony's strange judgmental
current below the surface, she was being
taken away from home from reality by a
wicked, evil backflow...now a man lay
wasted and smelly on the Arizona waste
land...for what? nothing.

You could die out here and never be
found, she thought and the first snow fall
would come soon and hide everything in a
peaceful white snow.

Alison tried to kill the pain and she hum-
med an old Navajo squaw dance song and
she saw in her thoughts the beautiful short
Navajo girls she grew up with in purple
velveteen dresses that drug to the ground:
all in a row, they looked like a wave of
water coming to meet the innocent land.

The roundness of their faces, their pretty
white teeth smiles that spoke of happiness.

She tried to listen to what they laughed about but they turned away from her. She opened her eyes and the sunshine was in front of them and she squinted and turned towards the open window and somewhere on the reservation between sage, cedar and muddy deep red canyons she felt a paradoxical pair that will always be good, evil--right wrong--truth beauty--Tony and Alison...

Can't get behind this mystery.
Thousands maybe more of shadows in the street lights. One night on the Manhattan streets homeless faces that get flattened out at night by brown cardboard box homes...some stand around like I've seen some Indian men stand around a campfire talking about the hunt. They talk about the fast life, the fast cars, the fast people in New York City who passed their own demons.

I passed a beautiful young Indian girl dressed in beat down clothes, pushing a shopping cart. We stared at each other for an instant her blood shot eyes screamed at me for something but I turned away too soon...the scream still echoes inside me and it settles to my thought of her raven black hair and I wonder what nation she ran away from...I walked through the thick smelly cement canyon walls of Manhattan Island until early dawn. Hold back the dawn, hold my dreams tonight...I want to

94

think of the girl I saw and in my mind carry a conversation with her...forget the formal introductions, her pretty face will follow me forever.

If I could lay you upon my ground and let you see the Mountain and smell the wild roses...My thoughts go away as a yellow cab screams down a one way street heading for an unknown passenger. The dark crevices of those grey canyon walls echo the sound of a gunshot from some ghetto on the East Side.

I turn the corner and get the shouts of a milk-crate preacher. He points to me, his big black finger penetrates my attention until I see his coffee can gimmick...and all I remember as my coat catches a northern wind are these words, "All the prophets that came before..." what a haunting thought. Maybe he is a prophet, a healer in his own right...Jesus we threw out into the streets because we didn't want to hear his words.

Now maybe this man this homeless hound that I turn away from could have been a holy man...I turn on this thought back to him, he was gone a ghost with a hoarse October voice that's now headed for the Harlem lights...on a magical flying cardboard carpet that settles on a crack-rush straight into a dusty little railroad town where he was born, where he first saw ravens fight for a bag of popcorn when the circus came one spring day.

In an old abandoned railroad shack on Dignity Road he caught his Dad raping a schoolgirl. He ran away with a fishing rod in his hands that day. There was going to be a change of season much too early. The grab-onto-the-moment attitude much too soon.

Silent in Manhattan my heart asks my God for a reason not an answer but a reason, my head looks up as I wait for a green light to turn red...

Did you ever see a catfish moon? Its life is short I hear and it sings its swan song early in the morning right before sun-up on the Delta plains, for catfish trollers...

Our wise leaders have made mistakes and those mistakes have become laws for re-born fools. My people grow no corn no more out here in this concrete land...

My leaders where will you stand on Judgment Day...you have covered up all the humble creations of God...and now you want to hide his children...they are in here in your streets, every corner, on your lawn they sleep...they spit-shine your limousine windows but you never give them anything. Come home to us your castle awaits you...I walked around from corner to corner from one street to the next, the sun shimmered on the forty-story buildings, shivering man crawled in between trash bins covered with the New York Times. I saw the homeless like zombies all night. I felt like an outcast in a land of foreign languages, in a foreign land.

My thought goes back to the girl with the raven hair as I climb into a warm elevator. I press twenty-ninth floor and the feeling of being in a roller coaster comes into my stomach as it goes up, up, above my friend who wakes up somewhere far below...her long beautiful Indian hair tangled up. My fantasy of her pretty face gets locked in Manhattan and I lost the key in the streets of this lonesome castle...I know the street, I've been down the old road but I know I'll never find it. And I know I'll never find her again the girl with the raven hair...tonight you will sleep on bed of flowers in my dream you will be the princess in the castle, not any more in my mind will you push your life on a one way street. Good day good night my homeless friend.

When I went into Franklin's bar, Friday afternoon, a couple of the Mohawks working on the Kalamazoo Street Skyline Bridge were talking about Fabian, a boyish faced, olive skinned, green eyed Narragansett-Irish boy, from Massachusetts. Kneecap said: "There's no way he could've made it alive...cement sets faster when it's wet..." Samson Littlefeather was thinking about Fabian's little boy, who was in a Massachusetts Indian hospital, down and out, getting chemotherapy. I guess that's why Fabian worked so hard--he had had a lot to pay for, in his soul. I told the boys I would call and tell his boy. I took a shot of that hard, Gypsy Hill gin and walked out from that warm bar, stepping into the cold, sleazy wind, that kept mentioning death with my every step. I put my hands in my pocket and pulled out a small writing that Fabian wrote about his girlfriend a couple weeks ago:

99

*The grass grows urgently, around concrete*
*buildings and everyone laughs and*
*compares nightmares in a New York*
*minute*
*I miss you when I'm gone from our home*
*sadness falls all over me, in the dark*
*alone in an empty room.*

I couldn't call the kid; I called Fabian's
brother in Minnesota. I guessed he could
carry the load from now on.

I walked to where the construction site was.
Just a skeleton of a bridge, still. I crossed to
the middle of it. A tugboat wailed a mournful cry, breaking the silence of the midnight
air. I couldn't believe just a year had passed since his girlfriend, Maybelline, had
killed herself.  Too many pressures--a rose
wilting away before its time. I can't say
much for Fabian: slipping on the ice covered rails is typical. His carabiner wasn't
even hooked to his belt, when he was
stepping over to the other side. Fell only

eight feet, head first into fresh cement,
where the pylons were supposed to go.
The cement was deep and like quicksand.
Hell, they saw him, they just couldn't get
there in time. Just the kind of freak accident
you read about on page eight. Makes you
want to think weird and crazy thoughts.
Maybe Maybelline pulled him in, and took
him away from the worries...I wonder how
long his boy is going to live; he has cancer
in the spine. Maybe the Good Lord needs a
young, happy family, in heaven, I don't
know.

I took out my last cigarette, crushed the red,
white, Winston wrapping paper, let it drop
from the bridge. It sailed down onto a tug,
ocean bound to greet a passenger boat.
The tug gave one more lonely cry, that
echoed through the steel boned, shivering
remains of the Kalamazoo Street Skyline
Bridge...

It's been ten years now, and Grandma's tired of fighting for her twenty acres of grazing land. She started in the winter of '77, when the sheep had no grazing land; she saddled her horse and took big sister Maria with her, and headed north, to the Four Corners area. The Colorado River was there, and Grandma had a hogan in a secluded spot. Her papa had made it for the summer grazing, but Grandma rarely went up there anymore. Her vision was heavy, and getting too hazy. Sister led the horse in the night, as Grandma sat quietly in the saddle. She would sing a song softly, every once in a while, and that kept Sister company in the dark. She had Rusty and Bleu, two well-trained dogs that took care of the sheep. A distant bark in the moonlight echoed in the snow-covered red canyon walls. Grandma got the two dogs when they were puppies, from a young Taos Pueblo dancer she met at the Gallup ceremonial. They loved the

high mesa winds, and had two litters of puppies in the cold canyons. Bleu was preg-
nant again and couldn't run with Rusty, so
she yelped every time she heard him chasing a stray. She stood by Grandma all the
time. Tonight, she followed the old mare
through the broken snow.

Maria got up with the smell of coffee and
Grandma's roll-your-own cigarette smokes,
that she got at the trading post. Grandma
told Maria to get up and listen. "What is it?"
Maria asked, "It's just a sheep getting
restless, Grandma..."
"No," Grandma said, "...something
threatening's happening...the snow isn't
pure and the smell is different in the
land...Let's go up to the top of the canyon..." Maria got up right away; must've
been important because Grandma's hair
wasn't even tied back yet. They wove their
way up in the icy canyon. They could hear
a humming in the earth as they got up,
towards the top. Grandma looked out, to

the west. It was Grandma's favorite place to go. Her father prayed up there. The sheep fed well on the top, and life was always fresh. Her father's fathers were buried in the old way, on top of these red canyons. But days sometimes never seem right and years were never the same, after Grandpa died. It was Grandma's favorite place to go, but today, all was poisoned. The sun and the sky seemed poisoned. Mountains of decaying dirt were piled, and giant metal animals were tearing up the earth. Pulling and dumping, digging and destroying... Metal giants with a tiny man in the heart of the destruction.

Sister brought Grandma home that night, tired and cold. The adults stayed up with Grandma, asking her questions about what had happened, about what they had seen, and Grandma told them everything. The next day, Daddy loaded the Ford and went to Shiprock, to find out from the government bureau what was going on. I knew

Daddy was mad, because he didn't take any of the children, except for me and big sister. They left Uncle Ronnie, to take care of the kids. There were twelve of us kids, including Uncle Ronnie's. Daddy was the oldest of eight kids, and he usually took everyone he could to town, when he went. Not this time. He didn't even sing Mama a song, as we left Navajo Mountain. In the morning he went to the edge of the road, said a quick prayer, gave an offering to the morning sun and said: "Let's go, no time to waste."

Daddy was in the Marines in the 60s, and he always thought that since the government had asked him to fight for his country, that the big men in the government would listen to him. But not this time, Daddy...they had another fight on their hands.

They talked to lawyers, official representatives, and even formed a group to stop the digging. For eight long years, they fought.

Daddy even told the government, the one that he no longer respected: "How would you like for me to go into your homes, and graveyards, and dig up your fathers and mothers, to look for precious coal?" The representatives just said: "We will pay you for what we have used..." They never understood Grandma, or Daddy, or the Navajo people. They kept on "buying" the land. They gave Grandma $327.72. Grandma said: "The land is not for us to sell, and I will never forgive them, 'til the day I die. The men who scratched the top of the red canyon and destroyed the people's prayers, destroyed my old age. I'm glad for one thing; that your Grandpa wasn't here, to see this happen to us..."

The government said it would benefit us; give us running water in our homes. There was nothing wrong with the way we lived. We used the water that flowed in the river, over by Cottonwood, but nobody drinks it anymore; they're afraid of all the ashes and debris, that fall on top of it at night. We need the water, so we go ten miles, to the nearest water pump to haul it back, in barrels. The government said it would benefit us, give us electricity. "We lived this long without it," Daddy said, "...and we're not going to get it. If you children want it, get it when I'm dead and gone, not while I'm here on this earth!" We felt the same way, us kids. The Weritos had electricity, they had light at night that was good, and they had a silver toaster, but no white bread to put in it; so it didn't make sense to me...just another distraction.

I got angry through the years, I guess because so many promises were made to Grandma that never came through. The government is still trying to fix the problem that it started. They stopped the digging on Grandma's land, but I hear they started elsewhere. They tried to water the land on top of the red canyon, but the land was old and frail when they started the scratching, so it's going to take them longer than they think, to rekindle life in the land that they destroyed. It's sad to think about the destruction. They did it just to see if there was coal or uranium.

Grandma's gone, buried in the old hogan in the red canyon. Daddy was forced by Mama and the younger kids to get running water and electricity. He was mad for about a year, but now likes to sit at night reading the <u>TV Guide</u>, watching wresting, and sipping an ice-filled cup of soda. Sister Maria is at the University in Las Cruces, studying about the earth. The sheep are all gone except for five of them, that we keep as pets. And old Bleu and Rusty are long past even being flesh, but their little ones keep barking down the road, at rolling tumble weeds that get caught by easterner winds, that get pushed deep into Daddy's barbed-wire fence. Some of the Navajo are part of the destruction, but me, I'm still fighting for the people, trying to get the government to stop the digging. I even went to Washington, to talk to the Senators. But in this mountain of paperwork and struggle, I sometimes wish that Grandma was still alive...I would load up the horse, get the dogs, take her up to the top of the red canyon, and have her sing me one more song, to keep me through the night.

It started in Hopi and it will make a full holy circle back to the Mother, back to Hopi.

Mateo Talayeva was seventy-three years old in 1981, when we met. I heard him mumbling something in his language as he said goodbye to his blonde white friends in suits and ties, leaving the L.A. airport. His thick hands grabbed a brown paper bag and I heard one guy say "...I wonder what in the world he'd say to the crumbling walls of Rome and Greece..."

He looked ancient with his long white hair tied back traditionally with a faded red ribbon. He turned to me and his bangs were cut straight across, and his abalone earrings reflected the sunlight shimmering through the tiny window of the airplane, and everyone looked out of place around him.

110

I had gone to visit my father's sister in Santa Monica for the July 4th holidays, and I was headed back home to Taos when I met Mateo Talayeva on the airplane, flying back to Albuquerque, New Mexico. I sat with him, introduced myself, and he said "Second time me sit in airplane, first time Friday. Me go back to Hopi." He told me it would rain hard. We sat quiet until the plane left the ground and L.A. was behind us. He said, "...the White Man's gods gone crazy..." and I slowly found out he spurted out comments, what he felt, in mumbling tones every once in a while at all the amazement he saw. His soft voice spoke and he said he weaved Hopi blankets and that's why the blonde guys in suits brought him out to L.A.. They collected Hopi blankets and they had a big show to honor him. He didn't know the men "...but they sure knew me..." he said. "I saw the ocean," he said, "...I smelled it, tasted it and felt the strength of it. My people came here for ceremonies..." he said; "...I stood naked on a rock in the morning sun, I prayed, gave offerings, thought of all the young men who came to get foam off the ocean a long time ago...I thought of how they picked it up with an eagle feather. I thought of the Anak'china dance, the Bringer of Gentle Rain in Sichomovi, their drums I heard, their bright kilts I saw, and the ocean sang their song. And when I got dressed," he said, "I saw three people sitting in a circle... the waves splashed them and still they sat." I wondered of the healing they got from these waters. I pictured him, his strong, small reddish body being massaged by the Pacific. He spoke again, "I had a little boy but he died. So did his sister. I buried them both and it was hard to let go of the blanket." He sat quiet. I asked if he had a wife. "I remember her."...his face turned toward the window and looked into the clouds. I ordered a Coke for him from the Barbie doll looking flight attendant. He held the plastic cup and spoke, "She wore her hair in the traditional butterfly whorls when she was young...soft skin and good hands. We sat together after gathering wood on the cliffs of Oraibi and talked about the sunset, how beautiful it was... later we spent time looking at <u>National Geographic</u> magazines and talked about the ocean, and ate late sweet water-melons. She left in the winter. Winter looks for the weak and old but she wasn't that old, just worked too hard."

Mostly we sat quietly from then on. I kept asking the wrong questions. I guessed he was alone, no more wife, no kids, probably just relatives. He weaved blankets, beau-tiful blankets I thought.

The captain of the airplane turned on the seatbelt sign and they picked up the plastic cups. I saw Mateo put his cup into his brown paper bag. The plane steadily ap-proached Albuquerque and in loudness of thunder it landed.

I told him I would visit Oraibi someday. He said, "Yes, come meet my family..." I gave him my address, maybe he could read, I didn't know; he looked at the paper and put it in his Levis pocket.

I helped him stand in line and a fat American man in first class pushed Mateo getting his coat. It made Mateo drop his paper bag and I heard a glass break and water seeped out of the bag. Mateo picked it up quickly, and I saw his face become lonely again. "Sorry," said the fat man, "let the stewardess clean up the mess, son!" He never understood what it meant to Mateo: first time he went on a plane, first time he'd seen the ocean and felt its power. Mateo had his ocean water in a mayonnaise jar to take to his holy lands to give to the Gods, and "sorry," said the fat rich man, "let the stewardess clean up the mess, son!"

Mateo had his nephew waiting for him and he spoke to him in his language and pointed to the fat man. I knew then to go to the ocean meant more to Mateo and the water was holy! I stopped them and told his nephew that I had brought ocean water for my Grandma to taste, and that he could have it. I pulled out a plastic container with sand and ocean water in it. Mateo looked to me and told his nephew something in his language, and his nephew told me that he was very happy and anything I needed he would do his best to get, and his nephew took my address.

Mateo was happy, happy to be back close to home, happy for the water. My folks were waiting for me also, so we said our fare-wells and that we would see each other again. He gave me the abalone shell ear-rings he was wearing. I held on tightly to them and saw him go down the big hall-way, and everyone looked out of place around him.

I never wrote to his family and his family never wrote me. I often think of Mateo. I see the abalone earrings. I wonder where he got the shell to make the earrings. I wonder about what he did with the ocean water. But mainly, I wonder if he's still alive in 1994 and if he ever got on a plane again...I doubt it.

It started in Hopi and it will make a full holy circle back to the Mother, back to Hopi